Andersen Press

THE GREAT BLACKPOOL
SNEEZING ATTACK

TIGER series

Elizabeth Hawkins	*Henry's Most Unusual Birthday*
Kara May	*Cat's Witch* *Cat's Witch and the Monster* *Tracey-Ann and the Buffalo*
Barbara Mitchelhill	*The Great Blackpool Sneezing Attack*
Penny Speller	*I Want to be on TV*
Robert Swindells	*Rolf and Rosie*
John Talbot	*Stanley Makes It Big*
Joan Tate	*Dad's Camel*
Hazel Townson	*Amos Shrike, the School Ghost* *Blue Magic* *Snakes Alive!* *Through the Witch's Window*
Jean Wills	*Lily and Lorna* *The Pop Concert*

BARBARA MITCHELHILL

THE GREAT BLACKPOOL SNEEZING ATTACK

Illustrated by Damon Burnard

TIGERS

Andersen Press · London

First published in 1993 by
Andersen Press Limited,
20 Vauxhall Bridge Road, London SW1

British Library Cataloguing in Publication Data is
available
ISBN 0–86264–404–6

Phototypeset by Intype, London
Printed and bound in Great Britain by
Mackays of Chatham PLC, Chatham, Kent

For Susie and Sally
(two multiple sneezers)

CHAPTER 1

Mrs Bossit's boarding-house was
the best in Blackpool – or so
everyone thought.

Geoffrey went every year with his
parents. But he didn't like it at
all.

8

Only Geoffrey knew what Mrs
Bossit was REALLY like.

She bawled at him till her face
turned purple.

She even made him scrub the hall
floor.

11

When he sang
cheerful songs . . .

. . . she locked him in the cupboard under the stairs. But nobody seemed to notice. Nobody cared.

What could Geoffrey do?

CHAPTER 2

One day, when Mrs Bossit went out to buy the week's supply of cabbage, Geoffrey hatched a plot.

He took a pair of her knickers and
a thermal vest off the line

. . . and sprinkled them with some itching powder.

All the next day Geoffrey watched
Mrs Bossit but her skin was as
tough as old boots.

Only once, did he see her scratch . . .

. . . and then she gave him a clip
round the ear for giggling.

19

In desperation, Geoffrey went
round to a joke shop on the prom.

21

'I've got some exceedingly powerful sneezing powder,' said the owner.

Geoffrey reached for his money.
The owner of the shop reached for
his glasses to make out the bill.

'Wait a minute,' he said, looking hard at Geoffrey.

Was this the end of Geoffrey's plan?

CHAPTER 3

He found his mother's wig . . .

. . . and he trimmed it with his boy scout knife until it was the right length.

Then he found a pair of very high heels to make him taller . . .

. . . and he borrowed his father's coat.

What a transformation! He looked
at least 30!

So Geoffrey went back to the joke shop in his brilliant disguise.

'Good morning, sir,' said the owner. 'Six packets of sneezing powder,' said Geoffrey in the deepest voice he could manage.

He took them and he pushed them
in his pocket.

Will Geoffrey's plan succeed at
last?

CHAPTER 4

Back at the boarding-house, Mrs
Bossit was doing her best to burn
a handful of fish fingers for
Geoffrey's lunch. She was doing a
good job, too. Never had fish
fingers been burned so well.

Poo!

Geoffrey slipped in through the front door and dropped his disguise quietly on the mat.

Then he tip-toed up the stairs to
her room and poured the sneezing
powder into a box of talcum
powder.

'LUNCH IS READY, GEOFFREY,' she yelled. (Why didn't she have a gong like other landladies?)

'Eat it all and eat it FAST!' she said.

What was going on at the boarding-house?

CHAPTER 5

Mrs Bossit had won THE BEST
LANDLADY IN BLACKPOOL
competition.
(Who could have chosen her?)

The Mayor was coming to present
the award that very day so she
dashed upstairs to get ready.

She wanted to look her best – so she had a good wash.
(She even did behind her ears!)

38

She dusted herself down with
talcum powder (or so she
thought) . . .

. . . and put on her favourite dress (which was like a spotted tent big enough for six boy scouts).

It was not until she was in the
lounge with her friends, that the
sneezing powder started to work.
Mrs Bossit nearly exploded!

The powder flew round like sand
in the desert

. . . and then the visitors started to sneeze and their faces turned the colour of tinned salmon.

What would Geoffrey do next?

CHAPTER 6

Geoffrey slipped out of the front door, and painted a warning sign.

DANGEROUS
SNEEZING
ATTACK
-
DO NOT
ENTER

Then he stood in the path of the
Mayor's car holding his hand out
like Superman.

'STOP!' he called. 'DON'T GO
ANY FURTHER!'

The Mayor was horrified when
Geoffrey told him about the great
sneezing attack.

Immediately, he called for help on his car phone.

'LOOKS DANGEROUS!' said
the head of the Emergency
Services.

Soon Mrs Bossit and her friends
were carried out of the house . . .

. . . and were taken to a safe place

– well away from small boys, fish
fingers and talcum powder.

They were locked away until the
sneezing stopped – which was
quite some time.

And what happened to Geoffrey?

CHAPTER 7

Geoffrey was presented with a
large gold medal for stopping the
spread of the Great Blackpool
Sneezing Attack.

He was cheered all the way down
the prom.

And the next day, he was given a special treat. He had Blackpool Fun Fair to himself. The Big Dipper . . .

and ice-creams . . .

the Switchback . . .

and chocolate . . .

the Corkscrew . . .

and candy floss . . .

the Bumper Cars . . .

and Blackpool rock

. . . until he turned as green as slimy seaweed and was sick all over his trainers.

It was the best day of his life!

Was all well for Geoffrey?

It was . . .

. . . until he reached into his
pocket for his handkerchief.

Unfortunately, one of the packets
of sneezing powder had leaked
just a LITTLE into that pocket.

But just a LITTLE was quite
ENOUGH.

Geoffrey began to sneeze and
turned as red as Blackpool rock.

The terrified Mayor called for
help.

Geoffrey was carried off struggling and sneezing and he spent the rest of the summer locked away. . .

. . . with Mrs Bossit.